The Book Tree

To Uwe, for never giving up on this one — P. C.

For my husband, Sina, who loves books, like Arlo — R. K.

Barefoot Books
2067 Massachusetts Ave
Cambridge, MA 02140

Barefoot Books
29/30 Fitzroy Square
London, W1T 6LQ

Text copyright © 2018 by Paul Czajak
Illustrations copyright © 2018 by Rashin Kheiriyeh
The moral rights of Paul Czajak and Rashin Kheiriyeh have been asserted

First published in the United States of America by Barefoot Books, Inc
and in Great Britain by Barefoot Books, Ltd in 2018
This paperback edition first published in 2020

Graphic design by Sarah Soldano, Barefoot Books
Edited and art directed by Lisa Rosinsky, Barefoot Books
Reproduction by Bright Arts, Hong Kong
Printed in China on 100% acid-free paper
This book was typeset in Centaur MT, Cut-Out and Liam
The illustrations were prepared in oil paints and collage

Hardback ISBN 978-1-78285-405-0
Paperback ISBN 978-1-78285-996-3
E-book ISBN 978-1-78285-440-1

British Cataloguing-in-Publication Data: a catalogue
record for this book is available from the British Library

Library of Congress Cataloging-in-Publication Data
is available under LCCN 2018008451

1 3 5 7 9 8 6 4 2

The Book Tree

written by Paul Czajak

illustrated by Rashin Kheiriyeh

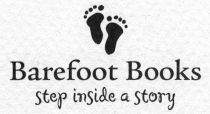

Barefoot Books

step inside a story

Nestled in the branches of a tree,
Arlo opened his book and breathed in.

Beginnings were always the best part.
They smelled as if anything were possible.

"I'm sorry, Mayor!
I got lost in my book
and it slipped."

"Preposterous! Books are
dangerous! I don't trust them.
They act like seeds, which
grow into ideas, and ideas turn
into questions. I will tell you
what you need to know."

First the Mayor gathered every book in the
library and then every book in the whole town.
Then he tore them up, until all that was left
was a single page that floated away
in a passing breeze.

Arlo chased the page as it blew across town. It reminded him of a dandelion seed drifting on a wish.

When it landed, the muddy earth swallowed it letter by letter until it too was gone.

Arlo thought that perhaps the mayor was right. After all, he'd been elected mayor. He must know something. But without books, Arlo noticed changes wherever he looked.

At school, teachers had nothing to read, so story time became
nap time. Without cookbooks, restaurants served only dry cereal.
No one went to the theatre, since actors had nothing to act out.
And in the place Arlo loved most, all the shelves were empty.

Arlo sat where the last page was buried. He missed the *crack* and *creak* of a book's spine the first time you open it. He longed for the smell and the crisp texture of a book's pages. But most of all, he missed getting lost in an epic adventure.

Sadly, Arlo scratched two words into the dirt. Endings were the worst part of any book.

But as he stared at the words,
they grew into an idea.

Arlo sat with pencil and paper
and let his ideas flow.

He read his stories out loud to anyone who passed by, but no one stopped to listen.

Then Arlo heard something.
A sound he thought he'd never hear again: that familiar *crack* and *creak*.

When Arlo looked for the source of the sound, he saw
a sprout springing from where the page had been buried.
It began to open its leaves. It reached for Arlo's words,
begging for more.

With every story Arlo wrote and read aloud,
the sprout grew. Arlo wrote a story about a giant,
and the tree grew tall, stretching for the clouds.

He wrote about a fire-breathing beast, and its
branches became as strong as dragon's claws.

He wrote about a magical swan made
of paper, and blooms of tissue paper
blossomed into books.

When the books were ripe, Arlo climbed
into the branches of the book tree and breathed
deeply, enjoying the fruits of his harvest.

While Arlo read, a friend stopped under the tree.
"I'm bored. There's nothing to do."

"You could try reading," Arlo said.

"Is that … a book?"

"Yup. Here, I love this story," Arlo said,
giving her a hand up into the tree.

The two shared the shady spot.

Soon flocks of readers roosted on the limbs. Books
spread through the town like pollen in the wind.

People grew hungry for reading again. Some wrote
their own stories and became book gardeners themselves.

Fiery maples bloomed with picture books, willows wept
with poetry, and fruit trees filled with cookbooks flourished.

As the trees grew, the town blossomed.

The mayor, lost in his mayoral work, was oblivious to all the changes. That is, until a ripe book fell on his head…

BONK!

The mayor kicked and stomped.
"Who planted these trees?"

"You did, sir," Arlo said. "When you
tore up the books, it planted an idea."

"Impossible! This is the second time
my head is hurting because of a book.
The trees have to be cut down."

"But we've become a town
of books and stories. You can't
cut them down."

The mayor walked the streets of the town. He gorged himself at one of the five-star restaurants, caught a show in the park and lost himself in a story about a boy fishing for a whale in a puddle.

"Books did all of this?" the mayor asked, astonished.

"No," Arlo said, as he handed the mayor a freshly picked story. "The book was just the seed."